Ravine Lereux

Ravine Lereux

A Supernatural Short Story

E. Denise Billups

Books by E. Denise Billups

Novels
   By Chance
   Chasing Victoria
   Kalorama Road
Short Stories
   Ravine Lereux
   The Playground
   Rebound

The raven bends infinity, casts light into darkness, and
Guides lost souls to their authentic selves.

"There is wisdom in a raven's head."
~Gaelic Proverb~

Contents

Cailleach

Beware the Cailleach, the veiled one
She's disguised in many forms
A beautiful enchantress
An old hag
And even a crow or raven
At will, she commands land and sea
Stealing skies with dark clouds
Enchanting forest misty, and
Unleashing winter's tempest
When ethers pause and ravens arise
You'll know she's arrived.
~E. Denise Billups~

*The Gaelic Mythology of Cailleach, pronounced (Kye-**luhkh**), is a divine hag, a creator and weather deity. A goddess of winter and spring, like the seasons she's ageless and infinitely renewed and believed to appear in many forms, even crows, and ravens. During times of war, she enchants with mist and forms dark clouds over battlefields. She's as ancient as history.*

Olivia
A Quarter Moon

"A QUARTER MOON … WE'RE SAFE." Olivia Lereux leans into the night and squints her green French Creole eyes at the two-sided moon—half dark, half opalescent. She sighs and tugs the plaid shawl about her thin shoulders, espying thick fog crowning Frenchman Bay, and Porcupine Island ahead. A view she and her brother Edward watched countless evenings on the porch in silence. Olivia lolls in her usual wicker chair, creaking beneath her delicate frame. She tilts her head, relishing the cool mist on her face and a trickle of herbal tea down her throat. The infusion soothes biting pain moving like microscopic volcanic ruptures along her arms and legs. A monthly ailment she's suffered since eighteen intensifies with old age.

"It's a quarter moon, Axel," she says, rubbing the top of her beloved chocolate Border collie's head.

Axel barks twice rises to his hind, and howls a double "A-rooo," that sounds almost human.

"Love you too," she says with a chuckle at his mimicry which he often does when directly spoken to. He lifts his wolfish yellow-eyed gaze and prods his nose into her side, a motion for a rub she gives reflexively with a double treat he loves, a scratch behind his ears. *My constant companion …* Without him, she'd be alone when work sequesters Edward for days in the laboratory.

Hmm, he's been gone a while … two maybe three days. She scours her memory, recalling she'd made apple pie on Saturday, three days ago. *Edward and that young man … What's his name? They ate several slices on the porch. Or was it a week ago?* Nonetheless, she knows he'll return. Olivia doesn't mind being alone on the cliffs, miles from town or anyone, except the Gibson family living apiece down the road. Occasionally, their son pops in after weekend hikes along the cliffs. A visit she welcomes with her prized Cortland apple pie and cider. She rakes her brain to evoke his name. *Brad … Ben … Oh, yes, Brent … Lovely man.*

An ebon cloud steals the moon, staining night onyx black. Olivia leans forward, sighting an unusual mass rolling west. Her thoughts wander. Darkness beclouds her mind once more.

Ravine
Sole Beneficiary

"WHAT HAPPENED TO THE FULL MOON?" Ravine ducks and looks past the windshield at a dark mass quartering the bright orb. *That's strange. Doesn't an eclipse happen during the day? Maybe it's just a cloud.* She reclines in the driver's seat staring at what's become a constant in her life—freeways. *Traveling again ...* She sighs ... *a wanderer just like my parents.* She's never stayed one place too long. An itch hits and she's gone—just her, the car, camera, laptop, and basic necessities. Now, she travels a familiar road, toward a place she swore never to return six years ago. But intuitively, she knew one day she would. For the same reasons that brought her to Covington Cove at seven-years-old, a similar fate calls her back. A family curse she once doubted, she's now starting to believe.

One, two, three ... she counts white 'through lines' to one-hundred then start again—a game to stay alert and keep worries at bay. *Futile ...* Aunt Olivia and Uncle Edward creep between twenty-five and twenty-seven. Soon, lines mesmerize, converging white waves on a tar sea. The car swerves. A horn beeps. Ravine drifts into the right lane, slows the car, grabs the Pepsi from the cup holder, and takes a tepid sip. Her fourth can.

A trailing car, races to the left lane beside her. The red-faced driver mouths angry words behind steamy glass. *Okay, buddy, calm down,* she wants to scream but doesn't, unequipped to handle road rage and a man twice her size. The car careens left and speeds away.

'LIVE FREE OR DIE.'

New Hampshire's motto displays on his license plate. *Well, he's free to speed right off a high cliff.* She smirks. A truck zooms past hauling its bloody carnage in the rear—two large bucks. "Bastards," she mumbles and looks away. The low fuel light catches her attention. "Shit," she swears, clapping the wheel. The tank's almost empty. Next gas stop, a mile and a half. *Will the car make it?*

She exits the freeway and follows the ramp toward Portsmouth, a quaint seaport town in New Hampshire. At the filling station, she rolls down the window and breathes in October's crisp, clean air. A young man races to the car.

"Full tank … regular, please." The stinging odor fills the interior. Ravine breathes deep and exhales a vapor she's always loved.

"That'll be forty-seven dollars."

"Cash, okay?" she asks, handing him crinkled bills.

"Thank you," he says taking the money.

A local diner beside the station appears a good rest stop. Ravine rolls the car into the parking lot and glimpses a reflection in the rearview mirror so like Aunt Olivia's, though the six-hour drive has dulled her skin and senses. A dab of gloss and powder does the trick. She tucks the snug cotton-blend Gap sweater, above her empty belly, into her skinny jeans, and exits the car. Lifting her head and tossing the black pea coat over her shoulders, she catches the full moon disguised as a crescent.

Inside the diner, Ravine slips into a booth, and a pert, thirtyish looking waitress appears pronto.

"Evenin', sweetie, what can I getcha?"

Sweetie ... I could be an evil bitch for all she knows.

The waitress pauses, chewing gum, pencil nub hovering over her pad. The unflattering crimson lipstick, bleeding below her thin lips, is wrong for her olive complexion. The tight bun makes her wide eyes look alien. Her potent perfume mingles with the scent of onions, fish, and chips wafting from the booth ahead. Ravine holds her breath and tries not to gag.

"I hope ya don't mind, but your eyes somethin' wicked beautiful. You get those green eyes from your muthah or fathah?" The inquisitive waitress asks.

"Thank you. My mom, I suppose, but it's a family trait."

"You look like those Creoles ... such attractive folks."

Those Creoles ... Some people just don't think before they speak, but Ravine detects she's just inquisitive, not an insensitive bigot. "And you would be right."

"I have a knack for that. Checkin' out folks in this place, make a long shift bearable. Hope I didn't offend."

"No, not at all."

"So whatcha' like hon?"

"A large hot chocolate."

"Anythin' else? We just made fresh batcha apple pies. Would ya like a slice or some wicked clam chowdah? We make the best in town."

No one makes an apple pie as delicious as Aunt Olivia's. "I'll try a slice of pie."

"Ayuh," she says, as the pencil rips across the pad with studied precision. "Be right back hon."

Ravine breathes deep, removes a crumpled envelope from her purse, and presses creases from the familiar paisley stationery. Uncle Edward's troubling letter came yesterday revealing she's the sole beneficiary of his and Olivia's estate. The unease that plagued her as a child, raced through her mind again, just like it had when she realized her parents were gone forever. The tone of the letter made her stomach lurch. She'd run to the phone, called home, and when no one answered the landline, she'd dialed Edward's mobile. After several tries, she'd panicked, postponed a photo assignment, packed her bags, and rushed to the car.

For years, she's prayed the Lereux family curse had taken its last victim, her parents. But now she worries the same fate has claimed her family once again.

Fifteen years ago, when her mother and father vanished, Edward and Olivia took her in. They became her sole guardians and now, she's their *sole beneficiary*.

Ravine,

I hope this letter finds you well, my sweet child. Attached, you will find two wills, mine and Olivia's. You're the only daughter we've ever known and love you like our own. Therefore, you are the sole beneficiary of our estate—land, home, and various investments we've made throughout the years.

The house is special to us. It's kept the Lereux's close to the natural environment they need. Soon you will come to understand who and what you are and appreciate the house as well.

Over the years, I've prepared for your return. In the cellar, you'll find years of my efforts. No explanation is needed. I've left instructions to guide you toward your new life.

If anything should happen to us, please take good care of Axel, he's a special pet to both of us. And don't forget to keep food in the birdcage for our feathered visitors.

Love You Always,

Edward

There's something wrong … Why would Edward send me this unless they're sick or expecting death? Ravine slides the second sheet of paper from the envelope and glances at the details of their will. She's always assumed she'd inherit their estate but hadn't expected a confirmation so soon. She's not ready to lose them, not just yet. As expected, everything is hers, even the house she swore never to return to. Their investment portfolio leaves her stunned. The modest life they'd lived as Research Scientists showed no hint of their wealth.

With Edward's final request to foster Axel, she fears something imminent, but they have more years to spend with their beloved pet. *Don't they?* She's never seen the three-year-old Border collie, but Aunt Olivia loves him like a child, not an animal. As soon as she retired, Olivia adopted Axel from a co-worker at the lab. After three years, Ravine still recalls Olivia's excited voice echoing through the phone.

"*Rave, say hi to Axel?*"

Axel woofed and howled through the speaker as Olivia coaxed him like an infant. "*He's such a good boy,*" she'd said in a sanguine tone. At the time, Ravine hadn't detected the subtle forgetfulness that would later steal Olivia's mind. She'd thought the occasional muddles were normal aging.

I should have been there for her.

After college, phone calls grew less frequent. Traveling often for work as a Nature Photographer calls whittled from once a week, to just once a month. And with the onset of Alzheimer, conversations were challenging. The last time she'd spoken to Olivia was a month ago. Her voice replays sorely in Ravine's memory.

"*Rave, something wrong? Why aren't you in class?*"

Ravine remained calm and stated in a natural voice, "Olivia, I'm twenty-two." There was dead silence. On other occasions, Olivia had forgotten Ravine's name, and once, hung up, believing a stranger dialed the wrong number. The strong, independent woman from her youth rendered vulnerable. Olivia's worsening mental state was and still is alarming and just as painful as losing her parents.

"Watch it!" rings sharply from the kitchen followed by a noisy crash, clatter, clank, and "Damn it!"

Ravine jerks her head toward the swinging kitchen door. The waitress exits, mouthing, "Shit," and wiping a bright, yellow stain from her clothing. She continues toward a customer, places his order on the table, and then sprints toward the restroom.

Ravine returns her attention to Edward's will and the storybook home she'd absconded for college. Returning to her family's beloved cliff-side cottage is difficult—a place that's always felt otherworldly haunted by something inhuman. As a child, she'd seen strange nightly occurrences. Events Edward and Olivia dismissed as dreams or tricks of the foggy cliffs. She knew they weren't, because she was wide-awake with the creeps, and could never fall back to sleep afterward. Six years later she's still uncertain. *Was it real or just fog drifts tricking my imagination?*

Ravine sensed her aunt and uncle kept many secrets. Olivia often said the "*Lereux's aren't normal people,*" and would augment that remark with a time-worn narrative about their French Creole ancestors which sounded like a mythical folktale. Animated, Olivia told the story of Aimee Darbonne and Henri Lereux in Creole tongue.

"*In 1854, a Scottish witch cursed our family. A Scottish woman spurned by a lover who fell madly in love with Aimee Darbonne, a beautiful woman from Saint-Dominque, our ancestor. When Henri Lereux took Aimee as his placée, the Scottish woman, jealous of the French Creole's beauty, cursed her and her progeny with the 'Cailleach.' The Placage, in New Orleans, prevented Henri Lereux from marrying Aimee. They left New Orleans traveling the Eastern Seaboard, always remaining close to forest and sea. They finally made the trip to Maine and to Covington Cove where they remained in the same home generations of Lereux's have lived. Aimee and Henri were common-law husband and wife and conceived three daughters and a son. When their first daughter turned eighteen, the curse began. Henri and Aimee vanished never to be seen again. Many reported seeing ravens wing over their home the night they disappeared."*

Ravine had always thought the story a fable, like many of Olivia's tales and often sensed she'd left out details. When asked why ravens appeared, she'd said, "Oh sweetheart, ravens are angels that guide souls someplace heavenly." Later she'd read ravens are symbols of dark omens and death. Olivia fibbed to allay her fears. With the Lereux family's dwindling numbers, Olivia's story may well hold some grim truth.

"When the time comes, the best place for people like us is sea-swept cliffs." Olivia's voice echoes. *What did she mean?* In some strange way, that place calls to Ravine.

When the time comes...

Ravine believes she knows what Olivia was alluding to. For four years, a change has stirred inside her flesh, growing, and yearning to be something other than Ravine Lereux. The subtle creaks whispering along her bones once a month are growing stronger. After each episode, Ravine wakes the next morning naked, her clothing strewn about the house, with no memory of what occurred.

She'll never forget the first time it happened and her ex's horrified expression. He'd launched from the bed, backed into and bounced off the wall, startling her awake.

"Tommy? What's wrong?"

"Rave," wild-eyed he'd stuttered, "look at your body!"

"What—what are you talking about?"

He'd ripped the sheet away from her skin and examined her like a doctor. Repulsion and confusion mottled his face as he'd cringed and crept away. "I saw it ... it was there."

"What was there?" Then, she'd felt her muscles relax and skin twitch. Something settled and retreated within her. She'd hugged her waist to control tingles moving along her inner core. Fearing her body and fright on Tommy's face, her heart and breath quickened. Something slithered, hiding inside as if it had sensed her horror. She'd tensed with its recoil.

Quickly dressing, with bulging eyes as if he'd just seen a horror movie, Tommy stammered, "I don't know ... Have to go." Rushing through the bedroom door, he'd mumbled, "I—um—I'll call you later."

He never did. Ravine phoned and left messages several times, but he never returned her calls. Whatever Tommy saw was terrifying enough to end a fourteen-month relationship.

Never again ... She'd vowed. *It's too painful getting close to anyone. Something's wrong with me, something others can see that I can't.* She senses it growing, trying to awaken. Instinct and her creaking bones tell her Aunt Olivia left out crucial information about the Lereux's.

She glares at Edwards words. *Soon you will come to understand who and what you are...* "What does he mean?" She mumbles. *What in damnation am I?*

Olivia
The Birdcage

AXEL SCRAMBLES FROM HIS SPOT AND BARKS INTO THE NIGHT. Turning his head, he barks again, fetching Olivia's attention, yanking her from that place she's stared for ten minutes. A triangular silhouette wings past her vision toward the human-sized, wrought iron birdcage Edward erected twenty years ago, with their feathered friend's recurrent visits every month on the full moon. A cawing cacophonous raven's dirge whelms the backyard, agitating and awakening Olivia's clouded consciousness. Again, she stares at the quarter moon. *They're five days early.*

Axel lopes to the porch edge, barks skyward, and then bares his teeth with a protracted growl.

"Axel, what's wrong boy?" Olivia rises from the chair, glancing at the gothic-style birdcage centering the garden like an iron vault. The overgrown garden, now thick with weeds, entwine with wisteria vines like dreadlocks climbing metal rails, and breeding a knotty gable.

I swear Edward pruned the garden a week ago. They couldn't have grown so fast. Well, at least the cage is preened and ready for guests. However, tonight, their early arrival has left her unprepared. *No eggs this evening my friends,* but the cage always contains cracked corn, mixed seeds, nuts, fresh blueberries, and water. Olivia stands dazed, mind adrift between past and present.

"Caw … Caw." Several birds soar over the roof. They rise into obsidian skies, bomb dive then glide inside the cage.

Olivia's enfeebled mind revives with worry. "We've got visitors tonight." Axel scoots under the wicker settee and growls at her. "Well, if that's how you feel, stay," she says perplexed by his reaction.

Olivia grabs the flashlight from a basket inside the kitchen door. Fearing breaking her withering seventy-year-old bones, she descends the porch stairs cautiously and waves the flashlight across the misty yard. Despite the stone wall circling the backyard's perimeter, Olivia frets about the rocky cliff flanking the cottage—mindful of the wooden stairway leading to the stony beach below and tumbling to an accidental rocky death. Her stomach knots. An image flashes in her mind then vanishes. *Something evil happened there*, but her memory fails her again.

Uncanny human-sounding chatter fades as she nears the iron dome. On entrance, Olivia gasps at the hushed cackle of ravens. Perched around the cage on iron rungs, they watch like winged sentinels—plumes black paint against waxen mist swirling round the cage. *Why so many tonight?* Nineteen she counts. They've never arrived together in such numbers, only when the full moon rises.

A vague sense of urgency tips her failing memory like a distant foghorn too far to detect, a whistle pestering her mind. *Have I miscalculated their arrival?* Doubt clouds her judgment. Lately, she's been so absentminded; it leaves her questioning her reality. Some days, she can't account for lost hours and often wakes with no sense of self or surroundings. Most disturbing was forgetting her age until she'd glimpsed her wrinkled hands or image in the mirror. Great agony arose with acute realization.

Another raven swoops into the cage. "Twenty," she whispers and scratches her head. She's surprised they're not feasting.

"Why aren't you eating my friends?" Their stillness rattles unease within Olivia. No feeding, fluffing of wings or jostling play. Tonight, they're unflurried. *Maybe there's a storm brewing or some natural event has caused them all to congregate so early*, she hopes.

"Tell me, my friends, what's the reason you've come so soon." Edward's voice rises from her waning memory. *"Remember the raven's arrival is an ill-omen."*

A day after Edward left, a curious raven with a white, striped beak appeared. Streak, a name she'd given the overfriendly raven, blinks its coal eyes twice and flutters from its perch around Olivia's head. She's never feared the large birds. From the moment they'd appeared, they've never pecked or clawed and took to her and Edward like old friends. She lifts her arm and Streak lands gently on her forearm. The bird croaks and rolls its head.

"You trying to tell me something, Streak?"

The bird's white-speckled beak reminds Olivia of a dapple of gray discoloring Edward's dark brown hair since birth. Streak flits from her arm and joins the tight huddle. Their focused gaze, planted on her, triggers more worry. Aware animals can attack without warning when they sense danger, she steps back.

Something's alarmed them. Is it me?

She roams the flashlight through cage rails, illuminating the overgrown garden. Searching wide and low, the only oddity she finds is Axel's absence. Normally, he runs around the cage sniffing and barking happy to see the ravens, but he's never wandered too close. Light shines through the kitchen window onto the back porch, spotlighting Axel's crouching posture.

"Grrrr," Axel growls at her with bared teeth, whimpers, and then scampers inside.

Alarm afflicts her senses. *He's never done that before.* Uneasily, Olivia exits the cage. "Eat and be safe tonight, my feathered friends," she says in a moderate tone. Creeping along the path and rolling the flashlight across the yard, the beam bounces off the carriage house's metallic window covers, speckling blackness beyond the stone wall.

"Cailleach!"

Olivia freezes. Uncertain of the voice's origin she casts the light in every direction. "Who's there?"

"Cailleach," resounds in her mind, loops around her, and echoes in the darkness.

She pivots, tossing light around the cage, the carriage house, the black cliffs … *Nothing's there except the birds.* She hastens toward the house, sensing eyes and eerie quiet pooling behind her. Not a stir. Rushing inside, she closes the door, and calls out, "Edward!" At once, she remembers she's alone, arousing even deeper alarm. She bolts the lock, dims the kitchen light, and wonders what spooked Axel outside. He always runs to his favorite spot for comfort.

"Axel?"

Inside the study, Axel's sagging, crimson cushion lies empty near the ebbing fire. A kindle pops and sparks as ash collapses in the wood-burning fireplace. She doesn't recall lighting a fire. By the window, a large full moon covers the computer screen; astral software Edward examines nightly, tracking the lunar phase. *Is Edward home?* She doesn't remember the last time she ran the program or using it tonight for that matter. A red text box alerts: *The software has expired. Renew subscription.*

A buzzing whirls like a beehive inside Olivia's head. She drops to the chair, eyes dazed, cheeks drooped, her mind stalled. The whirring whips about her brain, erasing prior thoughts, and the gathering of ravens in the backyard.

Ravine
Bah Hahba Waitress

"HEAH'S YA PIE, HON."

"Oh!" Ravine glances up with a start.

"Didn't mean to stahtle, ya looked miles away," the waitress says, placing the apple pie and hot chocolate on the table, and adjusting the too large charcoal-gray T-shirt she's replaced the stained shirt with.

"I was," Ravine mumbles, stuffing the letter into her bag, and sitting upright in the booth.

"Whah'ya from, hon?"

"Huh? Oh, everywhere … Well, I travel a lot for my job, but I'm originally from Maine. That's where I'm heading."

"How about that, I'm a Mainah, grew up in Bah Hahba. What part ya from?"

Bar Harbor, Ravine repeats and corrects the Downeast accent in her head with an inward snicker. She's lost the Maine slang over six years, but slips in and out on a whim, catching and correcting herself often. "Covington Cove."

"Ya out in the willie-wacks with all the crittahs, but it's beautiful. I used to hike Acadiuh nearby. Must get lonely though, not many folks in those parts."

"Acadia National Park is beautiful," Ravine says, recalling all the times she'd spent with Edward and Olivia camping, hiking, and kayaking. "It can be lonely at times," she agrees, "but you get used to it."

"I sahw somethin' creepy in Acadiuh once. Aftah a fright, I stopped hikin' alone. I haven't been theya in years."

"What did you see?"

"Whahevah it wahs, it wahn't human. Theya's this place called Hell's Gate my friends and I tried on a dahre—you know, stupid teens doin' stupid thangs. But that wahs the last time I visited that place. I cahn't tell ya what I sahw, but it wahn't a person or animal. It cast a large shadow ovah the grounds. We'd joked it wahs a monstah escaped from the nearby medical lahb up the way."

"It's a research facility. My family works there."

"Oh, what kindah work they do?

"Biomedical Research ... my aunt and uncle are Research Scientists and worked on regenerative studies, but they're both retired now."

"Regenerative, what's that?"

"Studies to reverse or slow the aging process."

"Too bahd they cahn't stop agin' altogetha. I could use a cure myself these days," she says patting the tight bun with a self-conscious titter. "So, ya headin' home to visit folks or movin' back?"

"Just visiting."

"Well, enjoy the pie and if ya change ya mind about the chowdah, just hollah my name, Maddie."

"I will, Maddie. Thanks."

Regenerative ... Ravine's always questioned Olivia and Edward's work. For a period, she'd thought their research involved natural cures because they'd always bring home strange green algae and make a nightly tea. A brew Olivia said kept them young and vibrant. She assumed they'd used the viridian tuft in laboratory studies and had no desire to ingest the stuff. One taste of the absinthian brew was enough. "One day," Olivia had said, "*It will help you feel better.*" Ravine assumed she'd meant if she ever got a cold or some minor illness.

Ravine catches 9 p.m. on the round retro style vintage wooden diner clock. Drawing the mobile from her purse, she dials Edward's cell and tries the house again. Still no answer. *They're always home at night.* Her appetite vanishes, but she needs something solid in her stomach with a three-hour drive ahead. She devours half the pie, unable to finish the rest. *Hands down, Olivia's pie is the winner.* Ravine gazes out the window at her dusty Jeep Renegade, imagining Edward and Olivia in severe danger, hurt, or worse, dead. She scoots from the booth with her hot chocolate, pays the cashier, and waves goodbye to the Bah Hahba waitress.

"Have a safe trip, now!"

"Thanks, Maddie. Take care," she yells, racing through the door.

Olivia
Cailleach Awakens

"CAILLEACH!"

Sensations of flight over water and jagged cliffs overtake Olivia. Vast wings clench about her frail frame and then unleash a horde of ravens. A bloody scream yanks her back to reality. Dazed, she glances around the study with no memory of how she'd gotten there. The last thing she recalls was sitting on the porch sipping tea and gazing at the quarter moon. *What time is it?* She glimpses the computer clock in disbelief. Straining her memory, only the porch and drinking tea comes to mind, nothing else. *What happened the last hour?*

A sticky note tacked to the computer, alerts:

READ YOUR JOURNAL.

She gathers her wits, opens the digital journal, and reads an entry she'd made when her memory began lapsing.

Beware of Cailleach. The onyx creature always visits on the full moon. Take shelter in the carriage house. Its steel-enforced walls and windows will protect you from the beast.

Olivia's certain she saw a quarter moon earlier, which means she has five days till the full moon. "I'm safe tonight, but best not depend on my faulty memory. I'll renew the software tomorrow," she mutters. *And there's no need to sleep in the carriage house tonight. I'll be safe upstairs in the bed where I've slept for thirty years.*

Olivia turns off the computer and walks to the door. "Come on Axel, time for sleep." Looking toward his cushion, she's surprised he's not there or underfoot. "Axel?" *Strange, where's he gotten to?* "Axel?" *Well, he'll join me when he's ready.*

Olivia flips off the lights, and heads upstairs. As she approaches her room, she notices her brother's bedroom door ajar. It's never open when he's gone. She checks inside, noticing the unusual disarray. *He's usually so tidy.* Sheets and quilts hang slipshod from the bed to the floorboards. One slipper rests in the center of the room, the other askew in the corner. Beside the computer, several books and notepads line the bed. He must be home. *Edward never leaves without his laptop.* She wanders inside his empty ensuite bathroom, then back into the hallway. "Edward?" *He's probably in the kitchen snacking as he does late at night.* But her aching bones are too painful to descend and ascend the stairs again.

Olivia heads to her room, hangs her head, and undoes the usual chignon at her nape. Strolling to the mirrored vanity, she drops three large bobby pins into a topaz-ornamented box. A gift for her eighteenth birthday from her mom the year they'd met the Lereux fate. Lazily, her eyes drift toward a glassy image, widening in disbelief. Her breath catches as she staggers back in horror. In the mirror, massive dagger-like wings unfurl like unclasping fingers, revealing a craggy, raven-haired woman. The antique-stained glass mirror quivers and swells. Spiderweb cracks splinter and shatter, exploding lightning-swift ravens from the woman's core.

Olivia swoops to her knees and covers her head, expecting the birds to rip her apart. Deafening wings charge the room, vanishing with a gusty whoosh. Olivia peers over her arms and raises her head, looking about the floor for shattered glass. Finding the floor clear, she stares up at the intact mirror with a gasp.

Was it just my imagination?

She rises from the floor and glances in the mirror again. A sharp breath swells in shock. A hag with gray, limp curls about her bony shoulders glowers back. Olivia raises her hands to her once smoothed brown skin, now spotted and crinkled. Beguiling emerald green catlike eyes are the only vestige of her waning youth and beauty. *Is it me ... am I this old? I look ninety not seventy. This can't be.* Disturbed and shaken, she throws her warm shawl over the mendacious mirror.

It's just my weary mind needing sleep, that's all. Ant-like twitches under her skin flame her fingers and toes. *The herbal brew...* Much too exhausted to trample to the kitchen, she undresses and crawls under the sheet, wearing only her bare skin. She wishes Axel was laying on the floor beside the bed as he does every evening. There's no sound of his paws or Edward's kitchen rumpus, only her rapid heartbeat and subtle, microscopic crackles beneath her skin. While Olivia slips into a deep slumber, an unkindness of ravens rallies in wait inside the birdcage.

Ravine
An Unkindness of Ravens

THREE HOURS LATER, AT MIDNIGHT, Ravine arrives at Covington Cove. The jeep meanders along several narrow roads and chugs up steep inclines ornate with autumn's birch and pine trees, toward the cliff ahead. Air dissolves thinner. Night alters. Dense fog swirls over treetops, creeps below, forming a diaphanous wall, dividing the road ahead. If she weren't familiar with the area, she'd swear the other side was nonexistent. A warm, wet October would explain the thick fog, but it's a crisp, thirty-eight degrees.

Swirling gauzy tendrils swallow the jeep, smothering views ghostly before freeing the car to finer mist. The incline flattens and then dips, revealing a dark mass drifting beyond a full moon over Frenchman Bay. The white cottage arises a surreal three-dimensional painting. Amber and tilleul heads tremble with the breeze, shaking foliage across the shadowy home. Windows shuttered laurel green, appear open-eyed, guarding the yard. The sun-bleached falcate timbered porch grins eerie in headlights.

Ravine parks the car alongside the slumbering home; praying Edward and Olivia are safe inside. Lowering the window, she gulps birch, pine, and sea-scented air, expels a prolonged breath, melting rising tension. Muscle twitches, besetting her since she left the diner, percolate along her feet and calves, and now dance about her thighs. Something within awakens, stroking and poking, effecting terror. She springs from the jeep and shakes her limbs, desperate to thwart what's rising beneath.

Immediately, a charge actifies the air, raising hairs on her arms. Affright, she stiffens and listens while shivers lace her skin. The paralyzing fear she'd felt as a child seizes her mind again.

It's happening.

An ominous hush falls as though ethers paused for its arrival. Ravine stares around the yard, wraps her waist in shivering arms and glances toward the backyard. Trembling leaves halt with quiescent breezes holding its breath... waiting as she has.

A growing need for truth surpasses her fear. *Proof ... the camera!* Instead of running inside the home for shelter, Ravine opens the jeep door and grabs the camera from the backseat.

If the camera captures it, I'll know it's real!

She removes the cap from her Canon EO5 Rebel, sets it to video, and treads on halting feet toward the backyard. A flutter rides silence around the dark home. A sound ever so slight, but discernable, always preceded the manifestation when she was a child. She envisions a gathering of watchful ravens perched rung to rung in the exotic birdcage, waiting for the creature's arrival as they had years ago.

An uncanny human cry sails from the backyard. Lifting the camera to her face, Ravine resumes an unsteady saunter. When she rounds the corner, an onslaught defies her next step, seizing her entire body. The camera escapes tremulous hands. Quavers attack her legs. She drops to her knees, contorting and roiling in pain. *It's never come so forceful.* She clasps her abdomen tightly to control whatever's ripping through her core. Her fingers ripple with ruptures opening her spine. Before blackness consumes her dwindling sight, a white-robed figure limping toward the birdcage crosses her vision. "Olivia?" The cage whirls black with wings gaining momentum. *They're ready.*

Olivia
The Onyx Creature

AS OLIVIA SLEEPS, A DARK SHADOW CREEPS ALONG HER SKIN. Her heart flutters like a trapped butterfly in her bony chest awakening her to a rash of sweat.

"It's here!"

Her breath comes fast with fear.

The carriage house…

Throwing a robe over her unclothed body, she shuffles downstairs and stumbles across the main floor. *It's coming too fast.*

Before she twists the doorknob, before she steps across the threshold, blackness slithers about her flesh. The onyx creature creeps like frost, inking her scalp, gray-white hair, brown skin, and green veins blue-black. The silky white robe twists and shimmies vaporously down Olivia's frail hips. The sash tangles her feet, sending her tumbling down mist-slickened porch stairs. A bone splintering scream rips the quiet night as Olivia rocks in agony.

There's no time to tend the broken tibia, no time to stop. *I need to get to the enclosure.* In the distance, bay fog drifts past the crystal crescent.

A full moon!

Olivia senses the blackness overtaking her soul. *I won't make it to the carriage house.* She crawls through dewy grass and then rises to a painful stand. Hobbling, she drags her broken leg toward the cage a few feet away.

The creature is swift, tugging, gripping, ripping, and contorting skin, muscles, and tendons like a fast-moving blaze. The raven's shrill caws mix with Olivia's shrieks as rapid twitches carve her flesh from spine to feet. Her soul withers void. Finally, escaping her diminishing frame, her robe sways and hovers ghostly in the air. With outstretched arms, she reaches for the cage. Just as she steps through the wrought iron gate, the knob slips through her fading fingers. The ground vanishes beneath her feet. The onyx creature seizes and carries her into the night, followed by ravens flapping and cawing close behind Olivia.

* * *

THE CREATURE WINGS PAST TWILIGHT over Porcupine Island. As quickly as it seized Olivia, it releases her prematurely, missing the slow-approaching jagged cliff. Feral eyes widen as the creature abandons her too fast. Feathered limbs stretch; talons widen and claw at the rocky ledge. A nail splitting, dust slinging scrap and screech follow a wild gust of winged arms grasping at nothingness. The cliff rises swiftly as wind whips past Olivia's body tumbling toward the rocky crags below. Wings spread and lift just before she impacts the boulder.

Ravine
The Last Lereux

A SHRILL CRY AWAKENS RAVINE to a moist tongue licking her face. "Axel?" *Olivia's beloved pet.* She bolts upright, glancing around in confusion. The dog barks, circles her, and then races toward the low-lying wall surrounding the clifftop. He stops and claws the ground with rapid paws, trying to dig a hole beneath the wall.

What's he doing?

Recalling the loud screech that woke her, she rises to her feet and walks toward Axel. In the distance, the sun tips the horizon. The entire night sped past her. *Did I sleep here all night?* She glances over the stone wall at an area with clumps of uprooted grass and rocks. Black feathers and scratch marks run to the cliff's edge. Axel barks again. He must have heard it as well. *It looks as if something went over the cliff ... but what?*

A breeze sweeps over the cliff, chilling her legs. At once, aware of her nudity, self-consciously, she clutches her body and races around the yard scooping pieces of clothing and dressing summarily.

What happened last night?

She remembers driving toward the house and exiting the jeep, but nothing else. Near the porch, her camera lies sideways on the ground. Wiping dust from the lens and checking for damage, she breathes relief. *Not a scratch.*

Pressing play, the paused video clamors with gruesome caws, grunts, and screeches. Ravine's eyes widen. She cups her mouth, silencing a sonorous gasp as fathomless images of Olivia morph strange in reverse—half-human, half-winged. Ravens swoop from the cage, circling and lifting her skyward. The pennate frenzy ascends dreamlike beyond the camera's view. "Olivia…"

In disbelief, Ravine stands trembling—her blood pulsing repulsion, and her head a tizzy of rejection. She sinks to the ground, drops her head, and hugs her knees into her chest. Tangled curls collapse about her face and knees masking a gush of emotions. She squeezes her knees tighter, wanting to crush her other half to nihility. Edward's words resound in her mind. *Soon you will come to understand who and what you are.* A sharp pang of realization charges her mind. *Edward and Olivia are gone … just like her parents.*

* * *

Ravine huddles on the damp ground several minutes staring beyond the cliff and stroking Axel's fur for comfort. Finally, she understands the monthly urge to flee, *or take flight is more accurate,* and the desire for forest and sea. It's in her nature. Words from Edward's troubling letter seize her thought.

Over the years, I've prepared for your return. In the cellar, you'll find years of my efforts.

Shivering from the crisp morning air, she stands and whisks leaf litter from her clothes and hair. Axel rises and follows her inside the cottage and down the cellar stairs. A pungent herbal scent permeates the basement. The same odor she'd smelled from Olivia's endless steaming kettle. She switches on the light, and a large room-length terrarium gleams with water-immersed algae. Around the cellar walls, shelves of glass jars bright with green fluorescent powder labeled, Lereux Algae inundate the room. In the corner, Ravine ambles toward a desk stacked with Edwards's notebooks and an envelope addressed to Ravine Lereux.

Ravine,

If you're reading this, Olivia and I are gone. Don't be sad, we've lived a long and happy life. Please, forgive us for withholding the truth for so many years. We wanted you to have a normal childhood and a loving home. Ravine you are a special young woman. You're the last Lereux and guardian of these blustery cliffs. Don't be afraid to embrace your Cailleach, the raven within. You have an extraordinary strength, channel it correctly and you will have a remarkable life as we have.

Here, in the cellar, I've left supplies of algae which will control your pain and subdue the creature. I discovered the algae in Acadia twenty-five years ago. While using it successfully in many regenerative studies at the lab, I also discovered the algae impedes and lessens the Lereux condition. Taken in small doses daily, this supply will last a lifetime. There's one caution. With age (roughly forty-eight) the algae's effect dwindles. You will need to increase the dosage when it does.

If you haven't already noticed, every full moon, you and the creature will become one. When the Cailleach appears, an old hag with a legion of ravens, you will know the creature's coming. The carriage house in the backyard is reinforced with steel. Take shelter there on full moons.

It's time for me and Olivia to join our ancestors, but we'll always be near. In Acadia National Park, there's a place called Hell's Gate, inappropriately named by locals. You will find a map on my computer to guide you to the spot. A heavenly place betwixt past and present, a place the guardian ravens reside and guide the cursed to their authentic self. You will find your family there.

Remember the birdcage, we will often visit.

Love Always,
Edward and Olivia

Someplace Enchanted

RAVINE FILLS THE STEEL BIRDFEEDERS with berries, seeds, water, and rakes autumn leaves from the cage. She's been home for two weeks, and strangely, doesn't plan to abscond. The moment she'd discovered her true nature, the creature cleaved securely to her essence. *This place, my home, is where I belong.*

Axel races about the cage barking at two ravens appearing daily since her arrival, resting on a rung above, fluffing their feathers and pecking at each other. In Olivia's journal, she'd discovered a passage about the raven named Streak. She's certain the raven is Uncle Edward and the green-eyed one Aunt Olivia.

"Hello!"

Ravine twists her head toward a young man about her age, dressed in hiking gear, wearing a backpack and an attractive grin.

"Ravine ... Rave?"

"Yes?"

"I'm Brent, Brent Gibson. Remembah we were in school togethah. Olivia used to bake pies for us. We ate right theya on the porch togetha."

"Brent, oh, yes, I remember. You've grown."

"So've you. It's good to see you back," he says, stepping around a mound of raked leaves. "Did Edward and Olivia leave for Floridah?"

She's relieved there's no need to concoct halfhearted lies. Edward's note explained he'd told the Gibsons and friends they're retiring to sunny Florida soon. He'd realized there'd be suspicions, especially given Lereux family history. Taking a gander at the cage, she throws a secret grin at two nestled ravens. "Yes, they've gone someplace enchanted."

The End

Dear reader,

We hope you enjoyed reading *Ravine Lereux*. Please take a moment to leave a review, even if it's a short one. Your opinion is important to us.

Discover more books by E. Denise Billups at https://www.nextchapter.pub/authors/e-denise-billups

Want to know when one of our books is free or discounted? Join the newsletter at http://eepurl.com/bqqB3H

Best regards,
E. Denise Billups and the Next Chapter Team

Acknowledgments

"No man is an Island," one of my favorite maxims and a true saying. Nothing's accomplished alone, and that's true as a writer and any other profession or aspect of life. I'd like to thank three extremely talented authors who've shown me what it means to give back to the writing community. Bebe, JDW, and JB thank you, my fellow Authors, for taking time from your busy schedules to provide critical feedback, insight, and inspiration in fine-tuning this short piece of fiction. You are a true blessing.

I'd also like to thank two special people in my life, my Aunt Ouida and Uncle Benny for their constant support and love.

About The Author

Imagine sultry winds, dusk, pitch-black, and haunting Alabama spirits, unseen in the cloak of night, whispering their stories. A familiar aura the Deep South carved into my youth before moving at the age of nine to New York City—a stark contrast to my natal roots. However, the south remains deeply rooted in my mind as I craft worlds from my city dwelling.

I'm an author with a rare mixture of Southern and Northern charm, born in Monroeville Alabama and raised in New York City where I currently reside and work in finance and as a freelance columnist. A burgeoning author of fiction, I've published three suspense novels—Kalorama Road, Chasing Victoria, By Chance, and two supernatural short stories, The Playground, and Rebound. An avid reader of magical realism, mystery, suspense, and supernatural novels, I was greatly influenced by authors of these genres.

E. Denise Billups
http://www.edenisebillups.com/

You might also like:

Clare in Marseille by Z.A. Angell

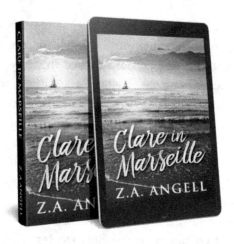

To read first chapter for free, head to:
https://www.nextchapter.pub/books/clare-in-marseille

CPSIA information can be obtained
at www.ICGtesting.com
Printed in the USA
LVHW020108131120
671492LV00002B/259

9 781715 694296